WELCOME TO

Collect the special coins in this book. You will earn one gold coin for every chapter you read.

Once you have finished all the chapters, find out what to do with your gold coins at the back of the book.

With special thanks to Allan Frewin Jones

www.beast-quest.com

ORCHARD BOOKS

First published in Great Britain in 2017 by The Watts Publishing Group

1 3 5 7 9 10 8 6 4 2

A CIP catalogue record for this book is available from the British Library.

ISBN 978 1 40834 321 0

Printed in Great Britain

The paper and board used in this book are made from wood from responsible sources

Orchard Books
An imprint of Hachette Children's Group
Part of The Watts Publishing Group Limited
Carmelite House, 50 Victoria Embankment, London EC4Y 0DZ

An Hachette UK Company
www.hachette.co.uk
www.hachettechildrens.co.uk

Beast Quest®

SKALIX THE SNAPPING HORROR

BY ADAM BLADE

QUARRY
SHARD MOUNTAINS
THE WATERS OF FORGETTING

THE ISLE OF GHOSTS
KATO'S CASTLE
THE
IGHT'S
KNOLL
FOREST OF THE LOST
THE MARSH OF MISERY

CONTENTS

They thought I was dead, but death is not always the end.

My body was consumed in Ferno's dragon-fire, though that pain is a distant memory now. I have been trapped in this place – this Isle of Ghosts – for too long. It is time for me to remind my old enemies of my power.

The boundary between the realm of spirits and the realm of the living is like a thick castle wall – unbreakable by force or magic. But every castle has its weakness – someone on the inside who can lower the drawbridge. And I have found him. A weak wizard, but strong enough to do my bidding.

Hear me, Berric! Heed my summons. Open the way for me to return, and I will show Avantia that Evil like mine is impossible to kill.

Malvel

RIDER OF THE GHOST WOLF

Tom stared into the empty space where the Dark Wizard Malvel had been standing only a moment ago.

"It can't be..." he said, gasping. "It's not possible!"

The sneering figure of his old enemy had vanished into thin air, but Malvel's parting words still rang in Tom's ears.

Welcome to my world... You shall never leave!

Elenna's eyes were wide with disbelief. "But Malvel is dead," she said. "Burned to ash by Ferno's fire."

"In this place, the dead have all the power," Tom replied grimly. "And if we don't defeat him here, he may find a way to return to Avantia." He gritted his teeth. "That must not happen."

The rocks rose up around them like shards of broken bone. The sky was full of racing clouds. The wind hissed and shrieked through the mountains.

The Isle of Ghosts truly was a

terrible place. The Evil Wizard Berric had opened a portal, and planned to bring back an army of Beasts to Avantia. Their old friend Aduro had warned them to stay away, but how could Tom do that? His own father Taladon had come to him in a vision, urging him to help. The words were burned into Tom's brain.

You must not fail. Avantia depends on you!

And so they had come, using the Amulet of Avantia and the Wizard Daltec's ancient spell.

Tom gazed out over the edge of the high cliff where they stood. *Berric's still out there*. Tom and Elenna had managed to stop the young wizard from capturing Zulok, a giant bird Beast. But Berric had escaped. Tom reached his hand into his pocket and took out the metal feather left by Zulok. It was a key that would open a portal back to Avantia. *But we*

can't leave Berric here – he'll find another key eventually and return to Avantia with his Beast army.

"Something's coming," murmured Elenna, interrupting Tom's dark thoughts. She was pointing into the grey sky, where a shape was hurtling

towards them through the clouds.

Tom's hand moved to the hilt of his sword. "Another flying Beast?" His battle with Zulok had been gruelling, and he wasn't sure he had the strength to fight off another Beast so soon.

He called on the power of the golden helmet, and squinted into the sky.

What he saw chilled his blood.

It was a giant black wolf, soaring towards them on wide, leathery wings. Tom had never seen this Beast before...but something about it haunted his memory.

With an ashen face, Elenna slotted an arrow on to her bowstring.

As Tom watched the Beast dip its wings and rush closer, he drew his sword. The wolf's mouth opened, his fangs gleaming like knives.

Elenna closed an eye to aim. "I'll fire a warning shot," she said.

"Wait!" Tom struck the end of her bow with his hand.

Elenna gave him a startled look. "What is it?"

Tom focused on a dark shape behind the wolf's shaggy head. "There's a rider," he cried, "seated between the wings. Do you see?"

"I do," said Elenna, as the flying wolf swept lower.

The figure astride the Beast's wide back was wearing a hood that shadowed his face.

"Could it be Malvel coming back already?" asked Elenna.

"Not if he's got any sense," said Tom, his fingers tightening on his sword hilt.

The giant wolf thumped on to the rocky ground. His long black tongue lolled from his powerful jaws. Tom could smell the strong odour of the creature's matted fur.

Tom raised his sword. "Show yourself!" he called to the hooded figure.

The person drew back their hood, revealing a noble face with a golden beard and swept-back golden hair. Tom's heart leapt for joy.

"Father!" Sheathing his sword, Tom ran forward as his father climbed down from the Beast's back.

"You are sharp-eyed, my son!"

Taladon said, with a wide smile.

Tom reached out to hug his father, but stumbled right through him.

"I would embrace you if I could." Taladon sighed. "But it is impossible."

Tom felt a weight sink through his chest. He smiled ruefully. "I almost forgot you were..." His voice faltered.

"Dead?" said Taladon gently. "I am, my son. And so is Gulkien." Taladon patted the winged wolf.

Now Tom understood why the Beast had awoken memories in his mind. *Of course! Gulkien was one of the first Beasts*. He'd read about the flying wolf in the *Chronicles of*

Avantia, though never in his wildest imaginings had he pictured anything so striking and so mighty as the ancient Beast standing before him.

Elenna came up to stand at his side. "Hello, Taladon."

Taladon smiled at her. "Greetings, Elenna. Thank you for keeping my boy safe."

"Father," said Tom, "why are you here?"

Taldon's face became stern. "My spirit stirred when I sensed Berric's evil plot. While he's loose in the Isle of Ghosts, upsetting the balance of living and the dead, I will remain."

Tom swallowed. "But what about Malvel? He is here too."

Taladon's jaw clenched. "My oldest of enemies. So that is why Berric opened the portal. Malvel is using him."

"For what?" asked Elenna.

"To return to Avantia himself," said Tom, as the truth dawned on him.

Taladon nodded. "The spirits on this accursed isle will draw the life force from the bodies of the living. You must not let Malvel get close to you or he will steal your strength and turn you to ghosts, trapping you here for ever."

Tom stiffened, horrified by his father's warning. "While there's blood in my veins, I swear I won't let that happen."

Taladon smiled warmly. "Good luck, my son. But now I must depart." Taladon climbed up on to Gulkien's back.

"No!" Tom cried, heart sinking. "Can't you stay?"

Taladon shook his head sadly. "No, Tom. Or my spirit will begin to drain your life force, as surely as Malvel would. The dead and the living are meant to stay apart." Taladon pointed to the Amulet of Avantia on Tom's chest. "When your Quest is done, touch one of the Ghost Beast's keys to the amulet. A doorway to Avantia will appear. The amulet will also guide you to Berric

– it senses the living in this desolate realm."

Tom laid the amulet flat on his upturned palm.

"Close your eyes and picture Berric in your mind," said Taladon.

Tom did as his father said, filling his mind with images of the pale-haired wizard. A strange tingling filled Tom's hand, flowing from the amulet and streaming along his veins. It seeped up his arm, the magic pouring through his body.

He opened his eyes. The amulet was vibrating on his palm, and a slender section was glowing like molten gold.

"Follow the golden thread," said his father, backing away. He raised a

hand in farewell. "Goodbye for now, and take great care, my son. Go now with my blessing and my pride!"

He swung his leg over Gulkien's shaggy back. The wolf Beast spread his wings and leaped high, catching the air, rising steeply and sweeping away into the clouds.

Elenna touched Tom's arm. "Are you all right?" she asked.

He sighed, heart aching, but pushed the feeling away. "I won't let my father down."

THE DARK RIVER

It seemed to Tom as though they had been climbing through the bleak hills of the Isle of Ghosts for an eternity. The wind howled. Above, the clouds writhed.

The golden thread on his amulet remained steady, leading them towards a narrow cleft between two spires of black rock.

How long will it take us to find Berric? Tom wondered.

Stepping through the gap in the rocks, he gazed out at a long hillside of tall brown grass. It sloped down to a wide, twisting river.

"At last!" he said as Elenna stood at his side. "I was beginning to think this place was nothing but stone."

They made their way down, through the rustling grass. The river crept along slowly, the water a dull brown colour.

The thin golden wedge in the amulet flickered from side to side. "I don't understand," Tom muttered. "Which way does it want us to go?"

Elenna leaned over his shoulder.

"It's like it doesn't know," she said.

"We could really do with a map right now," Tom said.

"But no mortal that set foot here has ever returned to tell the tale," replied Elenna.

Tom stared across the river. The landscape beyond rose in barren ridges, grim against the sky.

"There's a boat!" cried Elenna. She ran along the riverbank to where a small wooden vessel lay moored among tall rushes, with two oars lying inside.

Puzzled and surprised, Tom followed her. They gazed down at the boat. Its mooring rope had been tied around a large rock. Tom felt the amulet vibrate. The golden sliver was pointing steadily at the boat. He paused, waiting to see if it changed again. But the needle seemed locked in place.

"We have to get in," he said.

"What if it's a trap?" asked Elenna.

"Then we enter the trap with our eyes wide open," Tom insisted, climbing down into the boat. He looked again at the amulet. "It's pointing along the river now," he said.

Elenna frowned, but she loosened the rope from around the rock and got into the boat. It rocked gently on the water as they settled side by side on the wooden seat, taking hold of an oar each.

Tom shoved the boat away from the shore with his oar and the boat drifted gently out into the middle of the river.

They rowed steadily, the oars creaking and splashing softly through the brown water.

Did Berric come this way too? The amulet seems to say so.

The gloomy banks glided by under the leaden sky. It was as if there were no night and day in this terrible place – just an endless, dismal twilight. Tom's thoughts turned to Berric, waiting somewhere ahead, and Malvel lurking, ready to suck the life from them.

The boat rocked suddenly.

"What was that?" asked Elenna, holding her oar still.

A cold tingle creeped down Tom's spine. He leaned over the side, staring down into the sullen water. A stream of choppy ripples wound around the stern of the boat. Shadows moved under the surface.

A shoal of fish, perhaps?

Thud!

Tom felt the planks shudder under him and the boat rolled wildly. Something had barged into them from beneath the surface...

Something so big that it had almost tipped the boat over.

"A log?" said Elenna, though her face was pale with fear.

"Row faster," Tom urged. They began to heave on the oars, powering the boat away. Tom glanced over his shoulder. They had left the circling patch of ripples in their wake. If there was something down there, it didn't seem to be following.

Perhaps it was just a submerged rock...

"Your amulet is glowing," Elenna panted as she plied her oar.

Tom looked down. The golden sliver shone brightly. "It must mean we're closing in on Berric," he said.

Elenna looked over her shoulder. "And on some rapids!"

Tom followed her gaze. Ahead, the river churned and foamed. "Head for the bank before we hit them!" he said.

But the current grew stronger, gripping the boat and throwing them towards the rapids, faster and faster. Cascades of icy water gushed over the side of the small boat, lapping around their feet.

Tom took the other oar from Elenna. Using the power of the golden armour, he heaved them towards the shore, his face splashed with spray. But something snatched at his oar from beneath the water, and jerked it down. It caught on Tom's sleeve and before he could free himself, he tumbled headlong over the side.

"Tom!" he heard Elenna cry, before roaring water closed over his head.

Bubbles frothed before his eyes. A

frantic hissing and booming filled his ears. He struggled, trying to claw his way towards the surface.

Something grabbed his ankle from below.

Frantically, he stared down. There was nothing there. But he could feel invisible fingers grasping at his legs, pulling him into the depths. He let out a silent cry and swallowed a mouthful of water. Eerie, transparent figures came into view beneath him, tugging at his feet and legs, and swimming round him. Blank eyes shone in their pale, ghostly faces, and Tom somehow understood who they were.

Spirits of people who drowned here!

He couldn't see the surface, and no

matter how he kicked and fought, he could not get free.

I'm going to drown too!

But then a cloud seemed to drift over his mind, fogging his thoughts. He couldn't think properly. He felt confused.

Where am I? What's happening to me?

His fear and panic fell away, leaving only strange sense of calm.

It doesn't matter. Drowning isn't so very bad...

Actually, the water felt warm and comforting. He stopped struggling, happy to let the hands of the dead pull him deeper.

1

THE WATERS OF FORGETTING

He rolled on to his side, retching. Water spewed from his mouth. His lungs hurt.

A hand touched his shoulder. A girl's voice spoke.

"Tom? Are you all right?"

He sat up. The light was harsh when he opened his eyes, and the air felt like knives in his throat.

The girl's face slid into view, the hair short and dark, the expression frowning.

He clawed away from her, seeing a bow and a quiver of arrows slung over her shoulder.

She was armed!

"Tom, it's me – Elenna," the girl said, reaching towards him.

"I don't know you!" he shouted, scrambling to his feet, his hands knotted into fists, ready to defend himself. He felt dizzy. He needed to be in the water again – in the delicious, dark water. He tried to sidestep the girl, but she blocked his way, her arms spread.

"What are you doing?"

"I have to be in the river. That's my home!"

"No!" The girl's voice was a shrill cry. "You'll die!"

Anger burned through him. Why was she getting in his way?

"You can't fool me!" he cried. "Move aside!"

He shoved past her, desperate to reach the safety of the river.

She caught his arm, but he shrugged her off. The river was calling. Soon, he would be snug among the deep weeds and silt.

"Tom! No!"

As he was about to leap into the water, the girl flung herself on his back, driving him to his knees. He twisted angrily in her grip, shoving her down into the thick mud. He clambered to his feet and his hand came down on the hilt of a sword.

I have a weapon, too.

He drew the sword. It felt strange

and unwieldy in his fist, but he thrust his arm out, pointing the sharp end at her. "Keep away," he snarled. "I'll use this if I have to."

Her eyes were full of fear. "Tom – the river's done something to you."

He grimaced, irritated by her words.

She lurched unsteadily to her feet. "You're the Master of the Beasts," she said. "You must remember!"

He shook his head. "You're a filthy liar," he growled.

He turned, stepping into the water. It was warm around his ankles. He waded out, smiling – happy as the water lapped his shins.

"I'm coming!" he called. One more step, then a dive into the perfect darkness of the river...

He heard the girl's voice close behind.

"Sorry about this!"

A moment later, he felt a blinding pain in the back of his head.

He tottered, half turning to see the girl clutching a hefty chunk of a branch. Then everything went black.

Tom found himself on the Knight's Knoll in Avantia, gazing up at a fire-rimmed portal that hung in the sky like a gaping mouth. A hot wind blasted down, scorching his skin.

Something terrible was about to happen. His eyes fixed on the dim shapes forming in the dark hole in the sky. They rushed forwards, growing larger by the moment.

Tom let out a breath of shock as two huge creatures burst from the portal. *Dragons! One poison green, the other flame-red!* Both of them breathed fire as they circled the sky around the dark knoll.

"Vedra and Krimon," Tom gasped. "But I saved them ages ago!"

Another shape burst from the portal. It wore grey robes and in its great head was a single glaring eye. A whip cracked. Another Beast emerged – a lion with three heads. And then another – a massive vulture-like bird whose eyes flashed with death-rays. "Soltra! Trillion! Kronus!" cried Tom, reeling back, recognising Beasts he had fought and vanquished long ago.

More and more dead Beasts erupted from the portal – dogs and spiders

and birds and bulls – whirling around the sky like deadly comets, circling him. Closing in!

A voice rang out.

"Attack, my Beasts! Destroy him!"

I know that voice... Malvel!

The eyes of every Beast turned to him. Their mouths opened and the night filled with roaring and bellowing and screeching as they hurtled towards him.

Crying out in terror, Tom raised his sword as the Beasts fell on him.

Tom awoke from his nightmare, gasping for breath, clawing at the air.

He fell back, panting. He stared up at the grey sky. He realised with a shock that he was wearing just his underclothes.

Where am I? How did I get here?

He sat up. He was lying in long

grass by a river. A fire crackled nearby. His clothes hung on sticks pushed into the ground, drying in the warmth of the flames.

Elenna stood over him, the thick branch in her hands. "Must I knock you out again?" she asked. "Or are you better now?"

Tom blinked at her, not understanding. "What happened?" Memories filtered into his mind: fighting with Elenna, desperate to get into the river.

"There's something magical in the water," Elenna explained. "You forgot who you were."

Tom got groggily to his feet. "I'm sorry," he said. "I think it's slowly

wearing off now."

"Good," said Elenna. "Warm yourself by the fire – your clothes should be dry by now."

Tom dressed quickly, ashamed that

he had let the river's dark sorcery into his mind.

"Maybe we should have listened to your father," Elenna said. "The Isle of Ghosts is more dangerous than anywhere we've ever been." She looked anxiously at him. "You almost drowned."

Images of his nightmare flooded through Tom's mind.

Was it just a dream – or a dreadful vision of what was to come?

He strapped his sword belt around his waist. "Come on. We need to get moving. We've wasted too much time already."

Elenna nodded and passed him the amulet. The golden thread was bright and steady, pointing away from the river.

He began walking, but deep in his heart lurked an unspoken fear.

Would this terrible Quest be the death of them both?

DANGER
DESTINY
1

THE SORCERER'S NOOSE

Tom held the amulet on his palm as it led them away from the river across a bleak landscape of spiky grass and dry earth. The greyness of the unchanging sky was seeping into his heart, dulling his mind, sapping his spirits.

They crested a hill and found

themselves staring down at a deep marshy valley swathed in fog. The twisted branches of trees reached up out of the mist like clawing hands.

The golden thread was pointing into the heart of the dismal swampland.

Silently, they walked down the slope and into the dense, wet mist.

The ground oozed beneath their feet. Twisted trees loomed out of the thick fog like giant, broken statues. Their branches groaned.

Tom shuddered. "I can feel death all around me," he said.

Elenna glanced around with narrowed eyes. "I think this place hates us. It hates anything alive."

She was about to walk on when she stopped suddenly. "Listen!" she hissed, pressing a finger to her lips then pointing into the fog.

Tom heard it too – voices, coming closer. He stared into the haze, listening intently.

A cruel voice cut through the air, lifting the hairs on the back of Tom's neck.

"You have become powerful, Berric," it said. "I am impressed."

Tom's stomach knotted. *Malvel!*

"Now you must destroy the Master of the Beasts," Malvel continued. "But beware, many others have tried and failed."

"Have no fear, my lord," came

Berric's voice. "Seth, Petra and the others were not worthy of your faith." He gave a hard laugh. "Trust me – Tom will die."

We have to hide. Tom touched Elenna's arm and pointed to the branches above them. She nodded.

Tom crouched low, tensing his leg muscles, fixing his gaze on the branch directly above his head. Using the power of his golden boots, he sprang up, catching hold of the branch and boosting himself on to it.

He lay across the branch, then reached down and hoisted Elenna up on to a branch next to him. Tom peered down. Moments later, the misty shapes of the two wizards

moved into view. Berric's boots made clear impressions in the wet ground, but Malvel glided along behind him, his feet floating just above the marshy earth.

But then something even stranger caught Tom's eye. Faint trails of misty light were flowing from Berric's back and seeping into Malvel's chest…

Of course! Tom remembered his father's warning, how the dead would drain the life force of the living.

Malvel is sucking the life out of Berric, and Berric doesn't even know it…

Tom clambered cautiously to another branch as the two wizards moved beneath him, trying to keep them in sight.

There was an ominous creak. Elenna flashed Tom an alarmed look.

With a crack, the branch gave way beneath him. He lunged for another hold, but his fingers fell short. Flailing wildly, he crashed on to the thick, squelching ground, spraying up globs of mud.

Malvel spun around. "See what ripe fruit falls from dead trees!" he snarled. "Berric, it seems your time has come!"

Tom scrambled to his feet. Berric already had a ball of white fire in his cupped hands, the light sending ugly shadows over his leering face.

"Ensnare!" Berric shouted, hurling the shining orb at Tom's head.

Before Tom could draw his sword, the fiery ball exploded in his face. It fizzed with magic and spun out into a long, lithe rope. While Tom was still reeling from the burst of light, the rope wound itself around his body, pinning his arms to his sides, biting into his skin as he fought for breath.

Grinning, Berric strode forwards. He flicked his fingers, and Tom rose into the air. He kicked his dangling feet, struggling to break free of the magic bonds.

Berric glared at him. "Give me the key," he said.

"I don't have a key!" Tom gasped, straining to pull his arms loose. He could see Elenna creeping closer through the branches of the trees.

"I mean Zulok's feather," Berric said. "Give it to me, or suffer the consequences."

"Never!" Tom's lungs ached as the noose gnawed into his chest. If he could only get one arm free, he could reach his sword!

A second rope spun out from Berric's glowing hand, wrapping around Tom's waist, digging into his flesh. Berric waved his hand and Tom hovered closer. The young wizard's eyes shone. "Give it to me!"

"Try to hurt him and I'll kill you!" cried a defiant voice.

Tom glanced up. Elenna was perched above them in the tree, an arrow notched to her bow, and aimed at Berric's heart.

"Think carefully before you make your next move," Malvel warned Berric, in a soft voice. The ghostly wizard stood back, arms folded and an amused smirk on his face. Tom could see that Malvel's skin was already looking less pale, his body more solid.

"Berric!" Tom wheezed, the

magical rope squeezing his chest. "Don't trust him!"

Berric couldn't seem to see the light seeping from his body towards Malvel. His wary gaze flickered from his master to Elenna. He bared his lips, his face contorted with thwarted anger.

"You must act, my pupil," said Malvel.

"Can't you see what Malvel is doing to you?" Tom croaked, fighting for every word. "He's stealing your energy! You're going to die so that he can live again!"

Berric spun around, glaring at Malvel. "I do feel...weaker," Berric said uncertainly, staring at the ghost.

Malvel smiled and shook his head. "The boy is trying to deceive you," he said smoothly. "Don't be a fool! Prove yourself, apprentice. Take the key from him!"

Berric turned back to Tom, his face furious.

"No more tricks!" he snarled. He raised one hand towards Elenna, a ball of light crackling at his fingertips. "Your arrow will never reach me!" he shouted, his eyes fixed on Tom. "Give me the key!"

"Not while I live!" Tom replied.

"Then you will die," mocked Malvel. "Kill him, Berric!"

Berric's eyes narrowed and he raised his glowing hand, but then he paused. His jaw clenched. He looked over at Malvel. "Master, what he said...it isn't true, is it?"

Malvel's face twisted into a snarl. "You try my patience, Berric. If you won't kill the boy, I know something that can. Skalix, arise!" With a cruel laugh, the ghost of Malvel vanished.

"Malvel?" cried Berric, looking uneasily around himself. "My lord?"

A moment later, Tom's ears were filled with a deep rumbling noise away to his right. The trees began to shake. He stared in dread, as the swamp began to bubble.

Through the magic of the red jewel in his belt, Tom sensed anger and a bottomless hunger.

Ten paces away, the ground suddenly heaved, bursting upwards, spraying mud and filth. The air shook with a mighty roaring. A black shape reared up, as tall as the trees, wreathed in weeds and dripping slime.

Burning white eyes stared at them and wide jaws gaped.

Skalix had come!

THE BEAST FROM BENEATH

The Beast towered above the trees, breaking through the mist. The creature had a broad, heavy body, armoured with black scales. His forelegs were short and muscular, jutting from the sides of his body.

It's a monstrous crocodile!

Berric let out a shriek and backed

away, leaving Tom still hanging in the air, wrapped in shining cords. As if in reply, the giant reptile gave a deep bellow from his underbelly, which rumbled through Tom's body like a roll of thunder.

"Free Tom!" Elenna shouted at Berric, but the wizard seemed too terrified to move. Elenna fired an arrow at the creature, but it bounced off the Beast's armour.

Skalix began to stalk forwards, ripping aside trees with his claws.

Tom wrestled the ropes, calling on the power of the Golden Armour. But it was useless. He was trapped by Berric's sorcery, unable to reach his sword, unable to defend himself.

Skalix stopped a few paces in front of them, and Berric backed against the trunk of a tree. The Beast lowered his long head. Tom saw evil white eyes under heavy black ridges. The glare fixed on Tom and the massive jaws gaped as another deafening roar blasted out. The mist was driven away as a putrid stink engulfed Tom. He choked, trying not to draw a breath. A long black tongue licked along the Beast's dagger teeth.

Boom! Something hammered down into the ground behind the creature, throwing out shockwaves that sent the trees reeling. It was Skalix's tail! It ended in a great knobbed club, spiked with bony knives.

Skalix lifted his tail, swinging it back and forth, smashing trees aside, spraying mud and slime.

It's toying with us.

"Release me, Berric!" Tom cried. "Can't you see that Malvel has left

us all here to be killed?" He strained against the magic ropes until he felt that his heart would burst. "I can save us if I'm able to use my sword!" he shouted. "Berric!"

But the young wizard didn't seem to hear, staring at the towering Beast

with his mouth hanging open and his eyes bulging.

Skalix growled like an earthquake. The spikes of his swinging tail shredded more branches, then he drew back, about to lunge for Tom…

Elenna's high voice rang above the Beast's deep growls. Tom glanced up as Elenna leaped from the tree, crashing down on Berric and smashing him into the mud. Instantly, the magical ropes fell away from Tom's chest and he dropped lightly to the ground.

The Beast snapped at Tom, his jaws blocking out the grey light of the sky. Tom's sword was in his hand in an instant, and he swung out. The blade clashed against the Beast's teeth, and Tom somersaulted back, out of range. Tom backed away, boots sinking into the swamp.

I'll lead it away from Berric and Elenna.

The Beast followed him, white eyes wary. Tom heard trampling boots behind him and glanced back to where Berric was running away through the swamp.

"I don't think so!" shouted Elenna, tackling him to the ground.

Tom turned back to the Beast. He studied the oncoming creature carefully, seeking weaknesses in his armoured body.

Nothing obvious, but maybe the eyes.

Tom drew his shield off his back as he stood his ground, every muscle tensed for battle. Over his shoulder, he heard grunts and cries as Berric and Elenna wrestled in the mud. He trusted that his friend would get the better of their foe.

With a bellow that shook Tom's bones, Skalix darted forwards, moving with terrifying speed for all his bulk. Tom leaped to the side, as the razor teeth snapped together a hand's breadth from his face. With battle-honed reflexes, Tom smashed his shield into Skalix's long snout, then swung his sword, ignoring the bolts of pain that ran up his arm as his blade cut into Skalix's thick hide. Tom saw that the wound was shallow, though, and it only made the Beast angrier. Tom heard a low whistling sound.

It was the Beast's tail, whipping towards him! At the last possible instant, Tom brought his shield up to block the blow, but the force

lifted him off his feet and hurled him through the air.

He landed badly, twisting his ankle as he sprawled across the wet ground. He only just kept a grip on his sword and shield. His whole chest felt bruised.

Tom looked up at Skalix. Between the teeth and the barbed tail, it was difficult to decide which end of the Beast was more deadly!

Tom struggled to stand up, dazed and winded. His feet sank into the bog, which oozed up above his ankles, slowing him down.

Skalix's white eyes were on him, and the Beast's long tongue licked across his teeth as he stomped forwards. His tail thumped the ground, spraying mud and grass.

Through the red jewel, Tom heard the Beast's dreadful voice in his head. *I devour all life!*

"Not mine!" Tom shouted. But as he tried to pull his feet free of the swamp, he sank even deeper.

Panic surged through him. *If I can't move, I can't fight!*

Skalix rose on his hind legs, preparing for a great leap forward.

Tom reached down, quickly loosening his boots. Using every last ounce of strength, he jumped forwards, his feet coming free. He swung his arms as he soared above the Beast. He tucked his head down, turned in a nimble forward roll over Skalix's ridged back and landed feet-first beyond the lethal tail. He slipped, almost falling as the mud slithered under his bare feet.

Elenna was on top of Berric, striking the wizard with her fists, then Berric managed to fire a spark of white light, which hit Elenna's shoulder and blew her back. Berric scrambled away, but Elenna hurled herself after him, bringing him down in a swampy pool of brown water.

Tom heard a horribly familiar sound behind him. Instinctively, he flung himself flat as Skalix's tail scythed above him. There was a dull, crunching thud. The spikes on the Beast's tail had lodged in a tree trunk above Tom's head.

Skalix roared in anger as he thrashed and writhed to pull his tail free. Tom knew he had only a moment to act before the Beast tore himself loose.

He scrambled up, his feet slipping in the slick mud. But he dug his toes in and gained enough traction to leap over the Beast's head. Tom raised his sword, and stabbed the blade into the Beast's eye. Skalix let out a shriek of agony.

Tom gripped his red jewel and was about to tell the Beast to surrender, when a cry made him look up. He looked across the swamp, where

Berric had his hands gripped around Elenna's neck. The wizard's hands were glowing, and Elenna's body was shaking and crackling with energy. Elenna managed to punch the wizard across the jaw. Berric stumbled and dropped her, but released another bolt of white energy from his fingertips, which snaked through the air and hit Elenna's chest. She flew back, pinned to the trunk of a tree by cords of light.

Using the power of the golden boots, Tom charged over the Beast's scaly back, towards Elenna. He spread his arms out to keep his balance, as Skalix bucked, trying to throw him off.

Tom's eyes were locked on Elenna and Berric, as the wizard's magical energy shook through Elenna.

"Hurts, doesn't it?" cried Berric.

Elenna turned to Tom weakly. "Help me...please!" Her cry became

a strangled groan, and Tom watched with horror as his friend's body flailed and her eyelids flickered shut.

He leaped off the crocodile's back. The grey sky was blocked out by a massive shape swinging towards him – the spiked club at the end of the Beast's tail. Tom raised his shield just in time. *Smash!* Tom felt a force like a battering ram hit his shield. Tom was hurled back, his body numb, his vision clouded with black spots.

He landed in the mud with a *splat*. The massive crocodile bounded towards him. The monster swung his tail again, smashing it into a tree. The trunk splintered in half, and the upper part fell towards Tom. He tried to crawl away, but too late. He cried out as the trunk crashed down on to his lower half.

Agony blazed through his legs. Without a doubt, both were broken. He tried to shift the thick trunk with his hands, but the slightest movement almost blinded him with pain. He could hear Berric's cruel laughter, and tried to see Elenna, but the mass of branches from the fallen tree blocked his view.

Then he heard the thump of heavy feet. Skalix was crawling towards him, his wounded eye leaking thick white slime.

Tom heard Skalix's voice in his head. *Revenge! Revenge for the pain*

you have caused me!

Desperately, Tom scrabbled at the earth, digging his mud-spattered shield in to try and lever himself free. It was no use.

Closing in on him, Skalix hissed in triumph. Despair filled Tom's heart.

I'm going to die...and there's nothing I can do to help my friend.

NO WAY HOME

Tom clenched his teeth against the pain, and forced himself to think. His gaze fell on a long, sharp branch, just within reach…

The crocodile Beast loomed over him, his breath choking Tom's throat and thick drool dripping on to his head.

Tom lunged forward and tore the

branch off the fallen tree, holding it like a javelin. His legs screaming in agony, Tom twisted and flung the spear of wood at Skalix. It struck the Beast's wounded eye, sending the creature reeling back, shaking his long head. His scaly forelegs clawed the air and his tail hammered the ground.

Tom wedged his shield under the trunk and lifted. Stretching his muscles to breaking point, he felt the tendons in his back straining as he heaved.

The trunk lifted a fraction. Tom reached towards his belt quickly and grasped the green jewel of Skor, pressing it against his thigh. He winced as the power of the jewel drove into his leg, knitting the bones together, beginning to heal the injury.

But am I too late?

Finally Tom felt the strength return to both his legs. With all his might, he kicked out, lifting the tree off himself with his shins.

He lurched to his feet and stumbled forwards, desperate to get to Elenna.

Berric was still holding her by the neck, energy fizzing from his hand into her body. She was completely limp. With a snort, Berric tossed her into a pool of muddy water.

Tom felt a pure, blinding fury

overcome him. Roaring, he charged. The wizard looked up at him, eyes widening in shock. Tom slammed his shield into the other boy's chest. Berric flew back, crumpling to the

floor. Knocked out by the power of the blow, he lay still.

Tom grasped Elenna's collar and hauled her up out of the water. *Please don't be dead...*

But as he laid her down on a drier patch of earth, he couldn't tell if she was even breathing. Tom dropped to his knees, one hand pressing down on her ribs. For a moment, he felt nothing, but then her eyelids flickered.

Relief flooded through Tom's heart. *She's as tough as they come!*

Elenna sat up, sucking in ragged breaths. "You saved me," she said, gasping.

"I owed you. You saved me in the

river, remember?" Tom replied. "Can you stand?"

"I can do better than that," she said, fire returning to her pale features. "I can fight!" Tom grasped her hand and pulled her to her feet.

A fierce hissing shook the air. Tom spun around. Skalix was still clawing at the sliver of wood in his eye. It wouldn't be long before he managed to free it.

"How are we going to defeat him?" Elenna said.

Tom felt the amulet around his neck. "Maybe we don't have to." He pointed at Berric's still figure on the ground. "We've done what we came here to do. We stopped Berric."

Tom took out Zulok's feather and pressed it against the amulet. The feather exploded in a burst of silvery energy.

For the space of two fearful heartbeats, nothing happened. Skalix had pulled the wood from his eye, and was now turning to face them.

Then there was a sudden burst of sparkling lights. They spun in the air, forming a shimmering circle.

There was a crack like distant thunder and the disc within the ring of white fire turned black.

The token was gone – but it had opened a portal back to Avantia.

"Grab Berric's legs!" shouted Tom.

Elenna reached down, grunting from the effort as she caught hold of Berric's ankles. Tom snatched the unconscious wizard's arms and they lifted him from the ground.

"Throw him through!" Tom cried.

They swung the limp body and tossed it through the portal. Berric disappeared into the black disc like a sack of grain tossed into a granary.

The Beast bore down on them, roaring in a frenzy of pain and rage, his dreadful voice like knives in Tom's mind.

You belong with the dead! Skalix will rip you to bloody shreds!

"Go through the portal!" Tom shouted at Elenna.

"Not without you!" Elenna cried, gasping as she looked up at Skalix, who was looming high over them. Drool dripped from his sword-like fangs, his scales flickering in the light of the portal.

"Together!" said Tom. "Now!" They bent their knees and sprang forward, but Tom felt himself jerked backwards, straight away. The Beast had the hem of Tom's tunic between his fangs.

"Run, Elenna!" Tom yelled, as he was dragged away, desperately trying to wrestle his tunic free.

"Never!" Elenna cried, stringing an arrow. "While you fight, I fight!"

She loosed the string and the arrow sped towards Skalix's remaining eye. But the Beast jerked his head aside, and the arrow bounced off his eye-ridge.

Skalix let go of Tom suddenly and

he fell forward. As Tom looked back he saw Skalix lifting a foot the size of a cart, high into the air over his body. Tom rolled as the great foot came hammering down with bone-crushing force at his side.

Tom heard a fizz of energy and then silence. He realised with a tingle of cold horror what it meant. Sure enough, when he looked over, the portal had vanished.

Their route home had gone.

A creeping chill passed down Tom's spine.

We're stuck here.

The Isle of Ghosts would be their home for ever.

THE ULTIMATE SACRIFICE

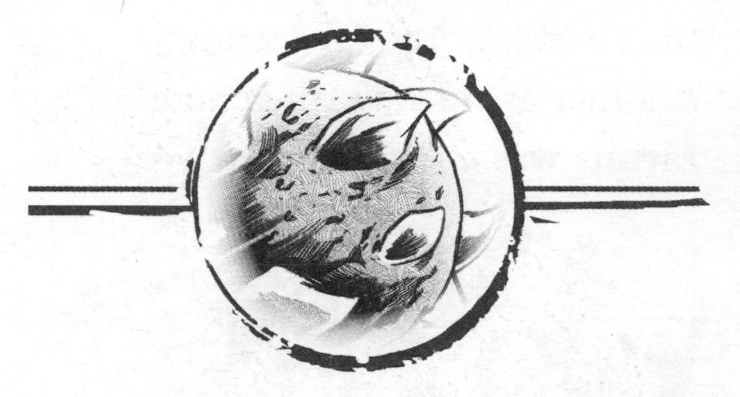

Tom turned back to the Beast, his energy sapped by hopelessness. Skalix's one good eye glared down at him, the slit of the pupil narrowing in triumph.

An arrow whisked past Tom's shoulder and embedded itself in Skalix's side – the point entering the Beast's flesh in the tiny crack between two scales.

Skalix twisted his body in pain, then cast his gaze on Elenna. Another arrow flew, then another. Elenna was aiming for the weak

points between the scales and some of the arrows struck home, while others bounced off.

"Aim for his eye!" Tom cried, keeping watch on the deadly spiked tail as it swung through the air.

If we can blind Skalix, the Beast will have to yield...

The barbed tail plunged down. Tom ducked and Elenna leaped back with a cry as the tail smashed down into the mire between them. A wave of filthy water and mud gushed into their faces. Gasping and choking, Tom stumbled back, blinded by the thick, stinking slime. He raced to Elenna's side.

"Watch out!" she shouted.

When Tom turned back, Skalix's raking teeth filled his vision.

Reacting instinctively, Tom lifted his shield arm and jammed the shield between Skalix's teeth, shoving hard, wedging it in the gaping mouth.

Skalix jerked his head, dragging Tom up, his arm still caught in the shield's handle. The Beast shook his head to and fro, flinging Tom from side to side. It felt as though every

bone in his body was being shaken, the tendons ripping apart.

His arm came free of the shield at last, and he was flung through the air. He crashed into a tree and thumped to the ground, his whole body throbbing.

Dazed and breathless, he hauled himself to his feet. Elenna was standing a little way from the Beast, firing arrows so swiftly that her movements were a blur. Some glanced off the scales, but a few dug into flesh. It only maddened Skalix further. It wouldn't be long before her quiver was empty too.

"Elenna!" Tom cried, but his warning came too late. Skalix's heavy tail swung around. Elenna bounded back to avoid the smashing blow, but the spikes caught her bow and ripped it from her hands.

Elenna tripped, falling backwards into the marsh, her remaining arrows scattered around her. Skalix rose on to his hind legs, his claws raking the air, the shield still lodged between his jaws.

No! He's going to crash down on her – she'll be crushed!

Tom flung himself forward. Gripping his sword in both hands, he raised it high above his head.

This has to work…

He closed his eyes, and willed the power of the golden breastplate to flow through his whole body. He felt his muscles tingle with magic. He brought the blade down swift and hard on Skalix's tail, which fell writhing into the mud.

Skalix bellowed in torment as black blood gushed from the stump. The Beast twisted around, his whole body shuddering, his single eye fixed on Tom.

Skalix lunged at him. Tom tried to run, but the Beast's claws raked across his shoulders, spinning him around and throwing him backwards into the mud. Tom struggled to get up, his shoulders blazing with pain.

Skalix's wedged jaws dripped stinking slime. A foreleg lifted, the claws like daggers, ready to tear Tom's body to bloody shreds.

THIEF IN THE MIST

Thwack!

The Beast suddenly lurched sideways with a grunt, and the long razor claws stabbed into the ground just a fraction from Tom's face. He stared up in surprise as the great body crashed down on to its side in the mud.

His shield fell from between the loose jaws and the long black tongue lolled out. The light in Skalix's one white eye dwindled and then died.

Elenna stood over the fallen Beast, the club-like tail end in her hands.

"Are you all right?" she said, breathing hard.

"I think so," said Tom, eyes travelling between his friend and the Beast.

If Elenna had followed Berric through the portal when I told her

to, I'd be dead now.

Elenna flung the weapon down and helped Tom to his feet.

"Thank you," he said, wincing from the wounds across his back. "You must have saved my life a hundred times by now."

Elenna smiled. "You've done the same for me," she replied. "Let's just say we're even!"

A strange gurgling noise erupted from the ground. The Beast was sinking into the mire. They watched as Skalix was reclaimed by the dark marshes of the Isle of Ghosts.

The swamp closed over the Beast. After a few squelching bubbles burst on the surface, it was still.

"I thought there might be another key," murmured Elenna, frowning.

As she said it, Tom saw something lying in a pool of muddy water. He plodded over on bare feet and picked it up. "There is!" he said, showing the thing to Elenna. It was a shell the same colour as Skalix's armoured body, about the size of Tom's palm. He pulled the amulet from his tunic. "We're going home!"

"Wait!" Elenna cried, grabbing his hand back as he was about to touch the shell to the face of the amulet. "What about your boots?"

Tom grinned. "I almost forgot about them," he said. "Maybe I haven't quite got over the effects of the river yet." He peered into the mist and spotted the upper edges of his boots in a patch of grassy mud.

Handing the token to Elenna, he made his way over to the boots. He drew them from the mud and was about to turn back when he felt a presence, like a freezing wind. Was it his father coming to say goodbye?

An icy hand caught his wrist, spinning him around.

Tom stared into an old, thin face, which was twisted in a sneer. "Malvel!"

The Dark Wizard loomed over him, mouth spread into a cruel grin. His cold fingers bit into Tom's flesh.

How can he be touching me? He's

just a ghost.

Malvel laughed in Tom's face. "Not so weak now, am I?" he crowed, twisting Tom's wrist. "Berric's life force helped me to become flesh again... But you, Tom – you will be the one who gives me back my full power! I will return!"

Tom staggered, gasping for breath as he felt coldness spread through his arm where Malvel touched him. His eyes swam as he fought weakly to get free. *He's sucking my life force from me!*

It was a horrible sensation – as though his very soul was being drained from his chest. Tom looked around for Elenna, but the mists had closed around him. He tried to cry out, but his breath seemed lodged in his throat.

"How do you like the feeling of death?" Malvel whispered, his eyes blazing with cruel power. "Did you ever think you'd be the one to bring me back? Avantia will soon bow before me once more!"

Tom reached for his sword, but his fingers were too weak to hold the hilt.

Malvel stretched out his hand and snatched the amulet from around Tom's neck. "Ahh, here's a pretty bauble!" he sneered. "You won't be needing it any more."

Tom heard a whistle and a thud.

The wizard jerked back, fingers slipping from Tom's wrist and eyes narrowing in pain. An arrow was sticking out from his arm.

"Just die, will you?" shouted Elenna, approaching with another arrow drawn.

Malvel snarled. He swirled his

cloak and vanished, just as Elenna's second arrow sped through the air and shot harmlessly across the marshland.

Tom dropped to his knees, gasping for breath. Elenna came bounding up to him. She lifted him to his feet.

"Thanks!" Tom said in a rasp.

"What was he saying to you?" Elenna asked anxiously.

Tom fought the numbness still tingling through his body. "It doesn't matter," he said, not wanting Elenna to worry more than necessary. "But he has the Amulet of Avantia."

Elenna looked despairingly at him. "So all he needs now is a token from a Beast and he will be able to return to Avantia," she said.

Tom straightened up and rested his hand on Elenna's shoulder. "I didn't mention it before," he told her, "but after I fell in the river, I had a nightmare. I was back at the Knight's Knoll. I saw a thousand Beasts rampaging over Avantia." He shuddered. "I heard a voice – I know now that it was Malvel's." He took a deep breath, feeling some of his strength returning. "Berric was just a pawn. If Malvel gets back to Avantia and releases all the Ghost Beasts, he will be unstoppable!"

Tom pointed to the black shell. "Give me the token," he said. Elenna handed it over. Tom drew his sword and brought the hilt down hard on the shell, smashing it to fragments.

"Now, Malvel will never be able to use the token to return to Avantia," said Tom. He held his sword high.

"I make this vow," he said, his voice echoing through the swamp. "We will not leave this accursed realm until we have destroyed Malvel once and for all!"

THE END

CONGRATULATIONS, YOU HAVE COMPLETED THIS QUEST!

At the end of each chapter you were awarded a special gold coin. The QUEST in this book was worth an amazing 8 coins.

Look at the Beast Quest totem picture inside the back cover of this book to see how far you've come in your journey to become

MASTER OF THE BEASTS.

The more books you read, the more coins you will collect!

Do you want your own Beast Quest Totem?

1. Cut out and collect the coin below
2. Go to the Beast Quest website
3. Download and print out your totem
4. Add your coin to the totem

www.beastquest.co.uk/totem

Don't miss the next exciting Beast Quest book, OKIRA THE CRUSHER!

Read on for a sneak peek...

THE FOREST OF THE LOST

Tom staggered through the endless reeking marshland, his back bent and his eyes to the ground. Mud sucked at his boots with each step and his sword and shield weighed him down. He glanced up to see

Elenna ahead of him, outlined against the dull red sky of the Isle of Ghosts. She turned and frowned at him, anxiously.

"Why don't we stop for a bit?" she said.

Tom shook his head. "We have to find Malvel," he said hoarsely. Since the ghost of the Dark Wizard had drained his life force, Tom had felt a coldness inside him, sapping away his strength. But he had to go on. Malvel had the Amulet of Avantia. That meant he only needed a key from a Ghost Beast, and he'd be able to return home.

And then he'll be unstoppable...

Suddenly, a strange mist swirled

up from the mud ahead of them, like tendrils of smoke caught in an eddy. The mist thickened into a twisting column, quickly settling into a familiar figure – a tall man with a golden beard and hair swept back from a noble face.

"Father!" Tom gasped.

Taladon's eyes were filled with pity. "Malvel will not rest until he has destroyed you, my son," he said. "And if you linger here too long, the ghost world will take you completely. Some Quests are unwinnable. There is no shame in admitting that."

Tom forced himself to stand tall. "It's not about shame, Father," he said. "I swore to protect Avantia from

Evil. I can't let Malvel return there."

Taladon bowed his head. When he lifted his eyes, Tom felt some of his strength return at the pride he saw in his father's gaze. "You are right, son," Taladon said. "I wish I could fight this battle in your place.

Instead, all I can offer is guidance."
Taladon pointed towards the dark treeline on the horizon. "The next stage of your Quest lies to the west. You must pass through the Forest of the Lost – a cursed place full of stranded spirits. Beyond the forest

you will find a fortress that Malvel has taken as his own – a stronghold from which he can subdue the Beasts of this land, ready to invade Avantia. Be careful, Tom. Malvel burns for revenge. He will show no mercy."

Tom balled his fists. "I have beaten Malvel before. I will beat him again."

Taladon nodded gravely. "I hope you are right." Before Tom could speak again, Taladon dissolved into shreds of mist that seeped into the earth.

"To the Forest of the Lost it is, then," Tom said, breaking into a run, Elenna at his side. Taladon's words had stirred a fierce determination inside him. As they ran over the barren plains, he let the rasp of his breath and the thud of his boots on the ground fill his mind.

Before long, the treeline loomed darkly before them. Gnarled and twisted trunks, leafless and blackened, rose from the grey, dry earth. Crows squawked at their approach and small shadows scurried between the trunks, making a chill creep down Tom's spine. Beside him, Elenna eyed the silver-black wood of the trees with a wary, almost frightened look. The cracked bark looked brittle and scorched, and the smell of stale smoke hung in the air. Tom felt a rush of sympathy for his friend. Elenna had lost both parents in a forest blaze – if she could be said to fear anything, it was fire.

"I'll understand if you can't go on," said Tom.

Elenna shivered, then raised her chin. Her eyes glittered fiercely in the half dark. "This fire burned out long ago," she said. "And even if it were burning now, I wouldn't leave you to face this battle alone."

Blackened twigs crunched beneath their boots as they trudged between the trees. Though the air was still, branches creaked and groaned overhead. From all around them, Tom could hear a whispering rustle, like the sound of leaves in the breeze, though every branch was bare. Within it, Tom caught snatches of words. "The voices of spirits," said Elenna, her face pale.

As they went on, the whispers grew louder, mixed with stifled laughter and muffled sobs. Elenna shivered and glanced over her shoulder, and Tom couldn't help doing the same.

He squinted ahead through shadows. At first, he saw nothing, but then he glimpsed what looked almost like features set into the trunks. He blinked, wondering if his eyes were playing tricks on him. With a sharp tug of heart-stopping horror, he realised they were not.

"The trees have faces!" he hissed,

catching Elenna's sleeve. They edged forward to a huge black oak. The ridges in the bark formed the unmistakable shape of a crooked nose. Below the nose, a splintered hole gaped wide like a mouth wailing in grief. Above, a pair of dark eyes seemed to gaze at them.

Tom shivered.

"Trapped souls," Elenna whispered, echoing Taladon's words.

They crept on in silence. Branches with long, twiggy fingers pulled at Tom's hair and clothes as he passed beneath them.

Elenna stopped suddenly, her head tipped to one side as if listening hard. "Can you hear that?" she said.

Tom listened, hearing nothing but the sound of their own breathing, and a faint rustling.

"Mother?" Elenna hissed. Her

eyes widened suddenly. "Father!" She leapt into a run, dashing wildly through the trees.

"Elenna! Stop!" Tom called. But she crashed onwards through the branches, quickly moving out of sight.

As Tom ran after her, his foot caught in a tree root, and he fell. He tried to stand, but the root had somehow coiled about his ankle, holding him fast. A rasping, hissing sound rose up all around him, making his scalp tingle with fear.

Read

OKIRA THE CRUSHER

to find out what happens next!

THEIR GIFTS MAKE THEM DIFFERENT
NICE HANDS!
FREAK!

BUT WHEN DANGER COMES…
CRACK!
RUMBLE!

SCREEECH!

…A HERO IS BORN

OTHERS WITH GIFTS WILL SEEK THEM OUT…

…AND SHOW THEM THEIR DESTINY.
EVER HEARD OF HERO ACADEMY?

OUT NOW!

TEAM HERO

TEAM HERO

TEAM HERO

TEAM HERO